Originally published by Spindlewood, Great Britain, 1990

Canadian Cataloguing In Publication Data
Bruneel, Etienne
  A whale of a bath

  0-88967-06706
  I. Holloway, Tess. II. Title
PZ7.B785WH 1990   j823'.914   C90-091461-0

Tree Frog Press Limited
10144 - 89 Street
Edmonton, Alberta T5H 1P7
CANADA

A Whale of a Bath

Etienne Bruneel

Story told by Tess Holloway

Tree Frog Press

EDMONTON

Would you believe it?
I had a bath the other day,

all by myself.

Would you believe it? A duck!

There's a duck in the bath with me!

Would you believe it? A frog!

A duck and a frog in the bath with me . . .
how extraordinary!

Would you believe it? A passing cloud!

A duck, a frog, and a passing cloud in the bath with me . . . most mysterious!

Would you believe it? A performing seal!

A duck, a frog, a passing cloud and
a performing seal in the bath with me . . .
quite ridiculous!

What now?

A fish!

More fish!

Wait a minute!

A WHALE!

No . . . No . . . No!

I don't believe it!

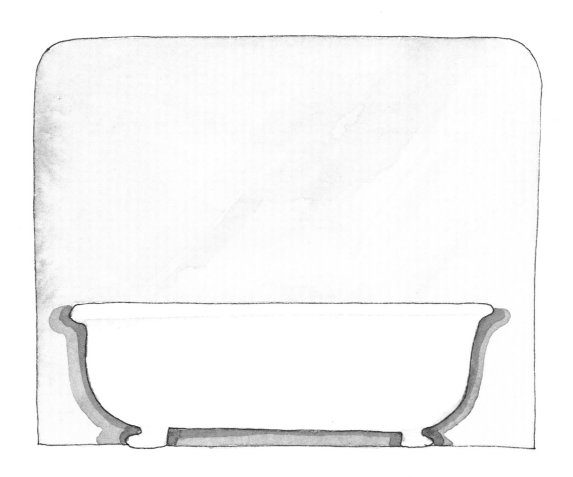

Absolutely no whale!

No fish!

No performing seal!

No passing cloud!

No frog!

No duck!

Just me in the bath . . .

all by myself.